this
·little·barron's·
book belongs to

....

....

First edition for the United States and Canada published 1999 by
Barron's Educational Series, Inc.

Copyright © Nicola Smee 1999

First published in Great Britain by Orchard Books in 1999.

All inquiries should be addressed to:
Barron's Educational Series, Inc.
250 Wireless Boulevard, Hauppauge, New York 11788
http://www.barronseduc.com

Library of Congress Catalog Card No.: 98-74978
International Standard Book No. 0-7641-0867-0

Printed in Italy

9 8 7 6 5 4 3 2 1

Freddie Goes to Playgroup

Nicola Smee

• little • barron's •

It's our first morning
at Playgroup.
I'm excited, but Bear's
a bit scared.

Tiny Tots
Playgroup

Mom says she'll be back very soon.

She'll pick us up when she's done her shopping.

Let's play with the water first, Bear.

Now I'll paint a picture.
This is much too messy
for you, Bear!

This is fun!

At storytime, I'm so thirsty
I have three drinks!

Then we all rush around...

except Dotty. She's too tired.

When Mom comes to
pick us up, I tell her
we've been fine!